How Cúchulainn Got His Name

This story was adapted by author Ann Carroll
and illustrated by Derry Dillon

Published 2012
Poolbeg Press Ltd

123 Grange Hill, Baldoyle
Dublin 13, Ireland

A catalogue record for this book is available from the British Library.

ISBN 978 1 84223 592 8

1

Cover design and illustrations by Derry Dillon
Printed by GPS Colour Graphics Ltd

How Cúchulainn
Got His Name

Also in the Nutshell series

One summer's day long, long ago, Cafad the druid came to King Conor of Ulster at his court in Eamhain Macha. The king was watching some swordplay between his Knights of the Red Branch and didn't want any distractions. But Cafad had seen a powerful vision and felt the king ought to know about it.

Barely glancing at the knights, the druid said, "Your warriors are famous and feared throughout the land, but the greatest of them all has yet to be born. I have seen him in a dream. He is Cúchulainn. He will bring honour to Ulster and his name will last forever."

The druid also knew Cúchulainn would bring much suffering as well as glory, but he didn't say this. I cannot change the future, he thought, and such knowledge is best kept secret.

In the months ahead no new-born boy in the province was named Cúchulainn and after a while the king forgot the prophecy.

Conor had a young sister, Dechtire, and he wanted a happy future for her.

One day when they were walking in the royal grounds, he asked, "What do you think of Sualtaim?"

Dechtire blushed, which was more revealing than her words. "He's all right," she said.

Conor counted the young man's advantages: "He's wealthy, handsome, strong and fearless. Would you agree?"

"I suppose so." Dechtire's face blazed.

"And he wants to marry you but, since you're not that interested, I'll put him off."

"No, don't do that! Sure I have to marry sometime, so it might as well be Sualtaim."

"Well, don't get carried away with enthusiasm," her brother said, thinking her face could now light a fire. But he smiled for he knew Dechtire loved Sualtaim.

But the sun god, Lugh, admired Dechtire's beauty and was jealous. At the betrothal feast, the god slipped a tiny, invisible, magical creature into her goblet.

That night she dreamed of Lugh. "Come with me to the kingdom of the gods," he whispered.

Immediately she was changed into a golden bird and followed Lugh to that magical Other World, near Newgrange, on the River Boyne.

Conor and Sualtaim were mystified by her disappearance. No one had seen her leave. Only Cafad, the druid, knew where she was and knew it was part of Lugh's great plan and that he would let her go in time.

After a month or so Cafed told Conor to look for his sister at the gates of the Other World, by the Boyne. They found her on the banks of the river, fresh from sleep and happy to see them. But she wouldn't speak of her time away.

Sualtaim was overjoyed to have her back and didn't care where she'd been.

The marriage went ahead and some time later Dechtire gave birth to a boy. They called him Setanta and thought him the most marvellous baby that had ever been born. Sualtaim loved the child but hated the rumours that went round Eamhain Macha.

"That is no son of Sualtaim's!" he heard.

"True. He is so radiant and strong! Lugh, the sun god, must be his father!"

Sualtaim couldn't stop the talk and so he took his wife and child to live far away from the court.

As a child, Setanta was always testing his strength: climbing the highest oak, riding the fastest horse, jumping the highest hurdle. But one day he realised he was bored and lonely.

I wish I knew other boys, he thought. I wish I had friends.

Then he overheard his parents talking.

"Soon Setanta must go to Eamhain Macha," Sualtaim said. "Conor will expect him to join the other boys there."

"It's too early," Dechtire said. "He's not yet seven."

"But you know he has strength and bravery beyond his years. And he will learn to use those qualities well in the boys' camp."

"Let him be for another year or two," Dechtire pleaded and Sualtaim nodded, always wanting to please his beloved wife.

But Setanta heard the words "boys' camp" and couldn't wait to find out more. He slipped away and over many days walked to Eamhain Macha.

He saw the sports fields first, where a fierce hurley match was in play. The boys were in their early teens and hurtled along, except for one player who was lazily waiting near the sidelines for the ball to come his way.

Useless! thought Setanta.

Charging over, he seized the boy's hurley, captured the speeding ball and scored a long goal.

At first the boys were stunned, but then Setanta took control of the game and, since he was on neither side, he scored goals for both teams and this infuriated them all.

"Look at him! Who does he think he is? Half our size and he's ruined the game!"

They turned on him and a mighty battle followed. Hurleys flailed, with Setanta giving better than he got. Since he was smaller he could slip between them then whack them on the leg or ankle.

Fergus Mac Roich, one of the Knights of the Red Branch, heard the fury and came running.

With great difficulty he restored peace. When the boys stopped roaring and he could make sense of what had happened, he turned to the stranger.

"What age are you?" he asked.

"Just seven," Setanta said.

"Seven? I think King Conor had better meet you. Not many seven-year-olds could beat two teams from Eamhain Macha."

At this the players looked shamefaced and the last of their indignation spluttered out.

Hearing the boy's name was Setanta, the king knew this was his nephew and gave him a great welcome.

And Fergus, who was much impressed by the child, offered to take him under his wing.

"I'll teach him. He can lodge in my quarters with Ferdia of Connacht and Conall Cernach. They're noble boys and suitable companions."

In time Setanta would outrun the fastest,
use his sword and spear with deadly accuracy,

defeat the best at chess, make the wisest decisions and be a true comrade-in-arms. And in Fergus's house he made his best friends too: Ferdia and Conall – brothers for life.

Some months after Setanta came to Eamhain Macha, the blacksmith Culann, who lived some miles from the court, invited King Conor to a great feast.

The smith had built his fortune by making sound weapons for the king's warriors, so strong any man using them felt invincible. And no horse shod by him would ever lose his footing or break a shoe. Culann was grateful to the king for his wealth and arranged the feast in thanks.

Conor set off in the late afternoon with Cafad the druid and his warriors. He spied Setanta in the sports field playing hurley.

I will ask the boy to the feast, he thought. Culann will be pleased to meet him. One day he will have to make the strongest weapons ever for him.

But Setanta wanted to finish his match and the king said he could come along later.

The smith was a generous host and filled Conor's goblet many times.

When the meal was ready, he said, "If there is no one else to come, then before we eat, Conor, I will set my hound to roam outside and be our guard.

He is huge and vicious – the best watchdog we could have."

"Do so – I've asked no one else," said Conor, forgetting Setanta entirely.

Meanwhile his nephew passed the journey to the smith's great house by playing his own form of hurling, whacking the ball into the farthest distance then running to strike it again while it was still in mid-air.

As he approached Culann's house the boy heard
ferocious snarling and growling. He caught the
ball in time to see a black shape hurtling towards
him, teeth bared, eyes burning, gaping mouth

ready to tear Setanta to pieces. The boy waited till the monster was ready to spring, then struck the ball with such power that it lodged deep in his throat, taking away his breath and killing him in seconds.

Inside, everyone heard the ferocious din and suddenly Conor remembered his nephew. Face pale, he led the charge outside. He was astounded by the scene, but not half as amazed as Culann who looked at the young boy and looked at the hound and made no sense of what he saw. He knew only that his great watchdog was dead.

Setanta saw the smith's dismay and under-
stood.

"From now on," he said, "I will take the
place of your hound. I will guard your home
until you find the equal of the dog I've killed
and my name will be Cúchulainn, or the Hound
of Culann, so everyone will know that I guard
what's yours with my life."

The king and Culann were mightily impressed by the boy's offer, but Cafad, who could see into the future, said, "If you take this name, you'll be the greatest warrior in the land and your fame will last forever, but death will come early and your life will have great troubles."

"I am Cúchulainn," the boy said. "If my deeds and name live after me I am willing to pay the price."

Cafad sighed. He knew that others too would pay a heavy price, that friendships and families would be destroyed. But he was a wise man and since there was nothing to be done, he said no more.

The End